Jack Kent's Book of Nursery Tales

Once upon a time

Jack Kent's Book of Nursery Tales

with text adapted by Polly Berrien Berends

Random House New York

To Polly,
who put the kettle on.

Contents

Goldilocks and the Three Bears

Once upon a time there were three gentle bears who lived together in a tidy house in the deep woods.

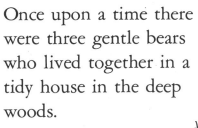

There was a great, huge father bear and a middle-sized mother bear and a wee, small baby bear.

Every morning the mother bear cooked a pot of porridge for breakfast and poured it into three bowls.

Then the three bears always went for a walk in the woods while the porridge cooled off.

3

One day while the bears
were out, a little girl
called Goldilocks happened
to find their house.

"I wonder who lives here?"
she said.

She knocked on the door,
but nobody answered.
She peeked in the window,
but no one was there.
At last she tried the door,
and it was unlocked.
So she walked right in
and sat down.

First she sat
in the great, huge
father bear's chair.
But it was too hard.

She tried the middle-sized
mother bear's chair, but
it was too soft.

Then she sat in the wee,
small baby bear's chair,
and it was just right.

But Goldilocks was too heavy for that chair, and while she was sitting there it broke all to bits.

Now Goldilocks was hungry, so she went into the kitchen and tasted the porridge.

She tasted the porridge in the great, huge father bear's bowl, but it was too hot!

She tasted the porridge in the middle-sized mother bear's bowl, but it was too cold.

At last she tasted the porridge in the wee, small baby bear's bowl. And it was just right, so she ate it all up!

5

Soon Goldilocks began to feel sleepy
and thought she would have a little rest.

So she went upstairs and climbed
into the great, huge father bear's bed.

But it was too hard.

She tried the middle-sized
mother bear's bed,
but it was too soft.

Then she tried the wee, small
baby bear's bed and found it
just right. And before long
Goldilocks had fallen fast asleep.

Now the bears returned from their walk in the woods. They could see at once that someone had been in their house.

"SOMEONE HAS BEEN SITTING IN MY CHAIR!" said the great, huge father bear in his gruff, deep voice.

"SOMEONE HAS BEEN SITTING IN MY CHAIR," said the middle-sized mother bear in her soft, middle voice.

"AND SOMEONE HAS BEEN SITTING IN MY CHAIR AND HAS BROKEN IT ALL TO BITS!" cried the wee, small baby bear in his squeaky, high voice.

Then the three bears went into the kitchen.

"SOMEONE HAS BEEN TASTING MY PORRIDGE," said the great, huge father bear.

"SOMEONE HAS BEEN TASTING MY PORRIDGE," said the middle-sized mother bear.

Then the wee, small baby bear began to cry.

"SOMEONE'S BEEN TASTING MY PORRIDGE AND HAS EATEN IT ALL UP!" he said in his squeaky, high voice.

Soon the bears went upstairs
where Goldilocks was still
fast asleep.

"SOMEONE HAS BEEN SLEEPING IN
MY BED," said the great, huge father bear.

"SOMEONE HAS BEEN SLEEPING IN MY BED,"
said the middle-sized mother bear.

"LOOK!" cried the
wee, small baby bear.
"SOMEBODY'S BEEN
SLEEPING IN MY BED—
AND HERE SHE IS!"

9

Now the wee, small bear's
squeaky, high voice
woke Goldilocks up.

She opened her eyes and saw the
three bears standing beside her.
And she was so frightened that she
jumped right out of the window
and ran home as fast as she could.

After that the three bears never saw Goldilocks again.
And it's just possible that they still live together
in their tidy little house in the deep woods.

The Little Red Hen

Once upon a time a pig and a duck
and a cat and a little red hen all lived
together in a cozy house by a blue pond.

Now the pig and the duck and the cat
were lazy and never did a stitch of work.
Every morning the pig waded into
his mudhole and wallowed there in the
gooey, squishy mud until nightfall.

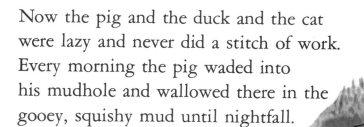

All the duck ever did was
to paddle about on the pond—
paddle and quack, paddle and
quack.

And the cat just sat in
the sun all day, sleeping
and licking herself clean.

Only the little red hen was not lazy. And because her three friends never did anything, she had four times as much to do to keep the house in order.

She was busy from dawn to dusk—dusting . . .

and sweeping . . .

and tending the garden.

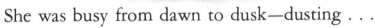

One day while she was scratching about for something to eat, she came across a few grains of wheat. She looked at her three friends, who were busy doing nothing as usual, and she had an idea.

"Who will help me plant this wheat?" she asked.

"Not I," grunted the pig from his mudhole.

"Not I," meowed the cat on her back.

"Not I," quacked the duck from the pond.

"Then I'll do it myself," said the little red hen. And she did.

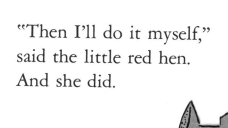

13

After a few weeks, the wheat grew tall and full, and the little red hen went to her friends again.

"Who will help me harvest this wheat?" she asked.

"Not I," grunted the pig.
"Not I," quacked the duck.
"Not I," meowed the cat.

"Very well, then I'll do it myself," said the little red hen.

And she did.

Now the grain was ready
to be ground into flour.

"Who will help me carry
the grain to the mill?"
asked the little red hen.

The pig rolled over and
grunted, "Not I."

The duck paddled by
and quacked, "Not I."

The cat opened one sleepy eye
and meowed, "Not I."

"Then I'll do it myself," said the little red hen.

Off to the mill she went with
a sack of grain on her back.
And home again she came with
a sack of fine white flour.

"Who will help me make this flour into bread?" she asked.

"Not I," grunted the pig.
"Not I," quacked the duck.
"Not I," meowed the cat.

"Very well," said the little red hen, "then I'll do it myself."

So she made up a batch of dough, and she shaped it into a loaf. Then she put it into the oven to bake.

After a while the delicious smell of fresh bread came floating out of the oven. The little red hen peeked inside, and the bread was ready to come out.

"Who will help me eat this bread?" said the little red hen.

The pig and the duck and the cat smelled the delicious bread, and they heard the little red hen, and they came running.

"I will!" said the pig, as he scrambled out of the mud.
"I will!" quacked the duck, as he raced across the pond.
"I will!" meowed the cat, as she rushed through the door.

"Indeed you will not!" said the little red hen.
"I found the grain and sowed it. I harvested it and carried it
to the mill. I made it into bread. And not one of you would
help me one bit. I did it all myself and shall eat it myself."

And she did.

The Three Little Pigs

Once upon a time there was an old sow with three little pigs. When they were nearly grown up, she sent them off to seek their fortunes.

The first pig that went away met a man with a bundle of straw. "Please, man," the pig said, "give me some of that straw to build a house."

The man did, and the little pig built himself a house of straw.

Soon, along came a wolf, who knocked at the door.

"Little pig, little pig, let me come in," said the wolf.

"No, no!" answered the pig. "Not by the hair of my chinny chin chin!"

18

"Then I'll huff and I'll puff and I'll blow your house in," said the wolf.

So he huffed, and he puffed, and he blew the house down and ate up the little pig.

The second little pig met a man with a bundle of sticks.
"Please, man," he said, "give me some sticks to build a house."

The man did, and the second little pig built a house of sticks.

Then along came the wolf. "Little pig, little pig, let me come in," he said.

"No, no!" answered the pig. "Not by the hair of my chinny chin chin!"

"Then I'll huff and I'll puff and
I'll blow your house in," said the wolf.

So he huffed, and he puffed,
and he puffed, and he huffed, and at last
he blew the house down and ate up the little pig.

The third little pig met a man
with a load of bricks.
"Please, man," he said, "give
me some bricks to build a house."

So the man gave him some bricks,
and the pig built a brick house.

Then, just as before, the wolf
came and said, "Little pig,
little pig, let me come in!"

"No, no!" answered the third
little pig. "Not by the hair
of my chinny chin chin!"

"Then I'll huff and I'll puff and I'll blow your house in," said the wolf.

Well, he huffed,
and he puffed,
and he puffed,
and he huffed,
and he huffed
and puffed,

but he could not make that brick house fall down.

When he found that all his huffing and puffing could not blow the house down, he thought up a way to trick the pig.

"Little pig," he said,
"I know where there is
a nice field of turnips."

"Where?" said the pig.

"Oh, in Mr. Smith's field," said the wolf.
"And if you will be ready tomorrow morning,
I will come for you and we will go together
to get some turnips for dinner."

"Very well," said the little pig. "I will be ready. What time will you come?"

"Oh, at six o'clock," replied the wolf.

Well, the little pig got up at *five* o'clock and went for the turnips by himself.

At six o'clock the wolf came to the pig's house and said, "Little pig, are you ready?"

"Ready!" answered the pig. "I have already been there and come back again. I have a nice pot of turnips for dinner."

The wolf felt very angry about this, but he said nothing. Instead he thought up another plan to catch the little pig.

"Little pig," he said. "I know where there is a nice apple tree."

"Where?" said the pig.

"Down at Merry-garden," replied the wolf. "And if you will wait for me, I will come for you at five o'clock tomorrow, and we will go together for some apples."

Well, the little pig jumped up the next morning at *four* o'clock and went off for the apples by himself.

He was hoping to get home before the wolf came. But it was a long way to Merry-garden and he had to climb the tree before he could reach the apples.

So it happened that he was still up in the tree when he saw the wolf coming.

"Ah, little pig," said the wolf. "I see that you are here before me. Are they nice apples?"

"Yes, very," said the pig. "I will throw one down to you."

He threw the apple so far that the wolf had to go away from the tree to pick it up.

While he was gone, the little pig jumped down and ran away home.

23

The next day the wolf came again to the pig's house.
"Little pig," he said. "There is a fair at Shanklin
Town this afternoon. Will you go with me?"

"Oh, yes," said the pig. "I will go.
What time will you be ready?"

"At three," said the wolf.

As usual, the little pig went off
ahead of time. He went to the fair
and bought a butter churn.

As he was going home with the
churn, he saw the wolf coming.

Quickly he climbed into the
churn to hide, and the churn
tipped over and rolled down the
hill with the little pig inside.

The wolf was so frightened by
this that he ran home without
going to the fair.

When the wolf found out it was the little pig who had given him such a fright, he was very angry indeed.

He went straight to the pig's house and declared that he would come right down the chimney and eat him up.

When the little pig saw what the wolf was up to, he hung a pot of water in the fireplace and made a blazing fire under it.

Just as the wolf came down the chimney, the little pig took the lid off the pot, and the wolf fell into the boiling water.

Then the wolf jumped up and ran away as fast as he could and never bothered the little pig again.

And the little pig lived happily ever after.

25

Chicken Little

One day Chicken Little was walking along when . . .

whack!
something fell on his head.

"Goodness gracious!" said
Chicken Little. "The sky is falling!"

"I must go and warn the king."

26

So he hurried away and he went along until he met Henny Penny, who asked where he was going.

"The sky is falling and I'm on my way to warn the king," said Chicken Little.

"It is?" said Henny Penny. "Then I better come along too."

So Henny Penny went with Chicken Little.

And they went along, and they went along . . .

. . . until they met Cocky Locky, who asked where they were going.

"The sky is falling and we're on our way to warn the king," said Henny Penny.

"It is?" said Cocky Locky. "Then I better come along too."

So Cocky Locky hurried away with Henny Penny and Chicken Little.

INN

POP

BILL

INN

28

And they went along, and they went along until they saw Ducky Daddles, paddling on the pond.

"We're on our way to warn the king that the sky is falling," said Cocky Locky.

"It is?" said Ducky Daddles. "Then we've no time to lose. I'll come along too."

So Ducky Daddles hurried off with Cocky Locky and Henny Penny and Chicken Little.

And they went along, and they went along until they met Goosey Loosey coming around a bend in the road.

29

"You better come with us,"
said Ducky Daddles. "We're
on our way to warn the king
that the sky is falling."

"It is?" said Goosey Loosey.

"That's terrible!"

Then Goosey Loosey hurried on with
Ducky Daddles and Cocky Locky and
Henny Penny and Chicken Little.
And they went along and they
went along until they met
Turkey Lurkey sitting under a tree.

"The sky is falling!" said Goosey Loosey.
"We're on our way to warn the king."

"It is?" said Turkey Lurkey. "How awful!"

Then Turkey Lurkey hurried to catch up with Goosey Loosey and Ducky Daddles and Cocky Locky and Henny Penny and Chicken Little.

And they went along, and they went along until they met Foxy Loxy, who asked them where they were going.

"We're on our way to warn the king that the sky is falling," said Turkey Lurkey. "Would you like to come along?"

31

"Indeed I would," said Foxy Loxy. "But you are going the wrong way."

"We are?" said Turkey Lurkey and Goosey Loosey and Ducky Daddles and Cocky Locky and Henny Penny and Chicken Little all together.

"Yes," said Foxy Loxy. "But I'll be glad to show you the right way. Just follow me."

So Turkey Lurkey and Goosey Loosey and Ducky Daddles and Cocky Locky and Henny Penny and Chicken Little all followed Foxy Loxy.

But Foxy Loxy did not take them to see the king at all. Instead he lead them straight to his den.

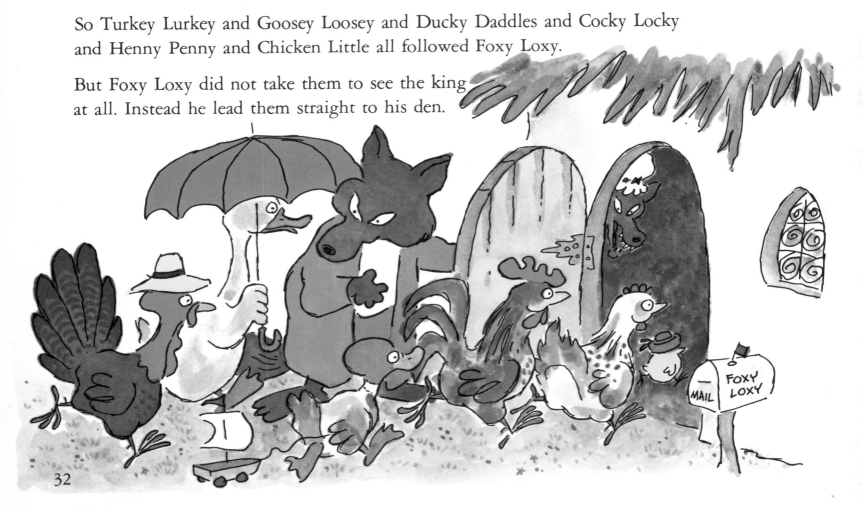

There he and his family had roast
Turkey Lurkey and Goosey Loosey and
Ducky Daddles and Cocky Locky and
Henny Penny and Chicken Little for
dinner.

So Chicken Little didn't get to tell the king that
the sky was falling. And, as a matter of fact,
the sky never did fall anyway.

Little Red Ridinghood

Once upon a time a little girl and her mother lived in a cottage at the edge of a deep forest.

The little girl had a red hooded cloak that her grandmother had given her. And she loved it so much and wore it so often that everyone called her Little Red Ridinghood.

One day Little Red Ridinghood's mother called her into the house and gave her a basket full of freshly-baked cookies and bread and tarts.

"Come, Little Red Ridinghood," she said. "Take this basket of goodies to your grandmother, for she is sick in bed.

"Stay on the path that runs through the forest and don't dawdle along the way. I shall expect you home in time for supper."

Little Red Ridinghood promised
to do as she was told and
started off through the forest.

She had not gone far when a wolf
stepped out from behind a tree and
stood on the path in front of her.

"Good morning, my dear," he said.
"And where are you going this fine day?"

Little Red Ridinghood was terribly frightened,
and did not wish to speak to the wolf.
But since he was standing in her way,
she answered as well as she could.

"I am taking a basket of goodies
to my grandmother who is sick in bed,"
she said. "Please let me pass."

But the wolf still stood in the
middle of the path. "And where does
your grandmother live?" he said.

"All the way on the other side of the forest," answered Little Red Ridinghood.
"So you see I really must hurry if I'm to be home for supper. Please let me pass."

At last the wolf stepped aside.

"Good day then, my dear," he said.
"I shall hope to see you again very soon."

Little Red Ridinghood continued on her way down the path. But the wicked wolf was not through with her yet. He had already thought up a plan to have both Little Red Ridinghood and her grandmother for his dinner.

SHORTCUT TO GRANDMOTHER'S HOUSE

As soon as Little Red Ridinghood was out of sight, he took a shortcut through the woods.

He ran all the way to Grandmother's house and knocked on the door before Little Red Ridinghood could get there.

"Who is there?" called Grandmother.

"It is I, Little Red Ridinghood," answered the wolf.

He spoke in a soft, sweet voice just like Little Red Ridinghood's. So Grandmother believed him and opened the door.

And the wicked wolf opened his enormous mouth and swallowed poor Grandmother whole.

Now the wicked wolf put on one of Grandmother's nightgowns, and her glasses, and a big ruffled nightcap.

Then he jumped into bed and pulled up the covers and waited for Little Red Ridinghood to come along.

He did not have long to wait. Soon there came a knock at the door. It was Little Red Ridinghood with her basket of goodies.

The wolf tried very hard to make his voice sound just like Grandmother's.

"Come in," he called in a high, quavery voice. "The door is unlocked."

So Little Red Ridinghood went in and set her basket down.

"Why Granny!" she said when she saw the wolf. "What big eyes you have!"

"All the better to see you with, my dear," said the wolf in his quavery Grandmother voice.

"And Granny, what big ears you have!" cried Little Red Ridinghood.

"All the better to hear you with, my dear," said the wolf, still in his Grandmother voice.

"And Granny, what big teeth you have!" cried Little Red Ridinghood as she began to back toward the door.

"All the better to EAT you with!" snarled the wolf in his own growly voice.

And he jumped out of bed and sprang at Little Red Ridinghood.

Little Red Ridinghood ran out the door with the wolf close behind her.

Luckily for her a kind woodcutter was just passing by.
With one blow of his great axe he killed the wicked wolf.

He slit him open, and out stepped Grandmother as fit as ever.

Little Red Ridinghood and her
grandmother hugged the woodcutter
and thanked him for his bravery.
Then they all had a picnic
from the basket of goodies.

And afterwards the kind woodcutter
took Little Red Ridinghood home.

The Gingerbread Man

There was once a little old man and his little old wife who lived together in a little old house.

One day, when the little old woman was baking gingerbread, she decided to make a gingerbread man.

She rolled out some dough and cut it into the shape of a man. She gave it two raisin eyes, and a saucy little smile of orange rind, and currant buttons down the front. Then she put it into the oven to bake.

After a while, the little old woman opened the oven to see if the gingerbread was done.

Much to her surprise, the gingerbread man jumped right out of the oven and ran out the door shouting,

Run, run as fast as you can.
You can't catch me,
I'm the gingerbread man!

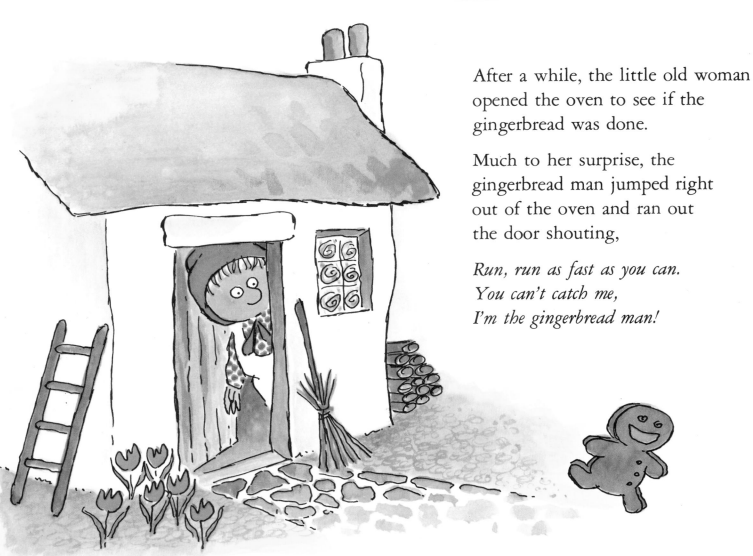

The little old woman ran after him,
but she could not catch him.

Soon the gingerbread man and the
old woman came to the place where
the little old man was chopping wood.

The little old man called, "Stop! Stop!"

But the gingerbread man just laughed and sang out,

Run, run as fast as you can.
You can't catch me,
I'm the gingerbread man!
And I can run from you, I can!

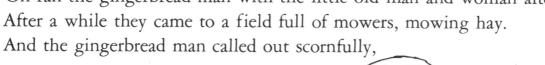

On ran the gingerbread man with the little old man and woman after him.
After a while they came to a field full of mowers, mowing hay.
And the gingerbread man called out scornfully,

Run, run as fast as you can.
You can't catch me,
I'm the gingerbread man!

I've run away
from a little old woman
and a little old man.

And I can run from you, I can!

He ran on with the little old man and woman and the field full of mowers after him.

But they could not catch him.

Before long they came to a cow,
chewing her cud. And the saucy
little gingerbread man sang out,

Run, run as fast as you can.
You can't catch me,
I'm the gingerbread man.
I've run away from a little old woman
and a little old man
and a field full of mowers.
And I can run from you, I can!

So the cow galloped after
the gingerbread man.

But she couldn't catch him either.

Soon they came to a pig, and
the gingerbread man cried,

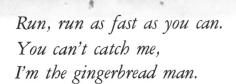

Run, run as fast as you can.
You can't catch me,
I'm the gingerbread man.

I've run away from a little old woman
and a little old man . . .

*and a field full of mowers
and a cow.*

And I can run from you, I can!

So the fat pig ran as fast as he could

and couldn't catch him.

Next the gingerbread man came to a fox, who looked at him out of sly eyes. And the gingerbread man laughed and sang out,

Run, run as fast as you can.
You can't catch me,
I'm the gingerbread man.
I've run away from a little old woman
and a little old man
and a field full of mowers
and a cow
and a pig.
And I can run from you, I can.

But the fox *didn't* run after the gingerbread man.

"I don't want to catch you," he said. "But there is a river up ahead which you cannot cross. If you like I will help you out by giving you a ride across on my bushy tail."

49

The gingerbread man took one look at the river ahead and at the little old man and woman and the mowers and the cow and the pig behind him, and he decided that the fox's plan was a good one.

So the fox jumped into the river, and the gingerbread man jumped onto the fox's tail.

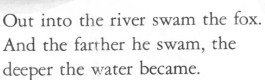

Out into the river swam the fox. And the farther he swam, the deeper the water became.

"Hop up higher or you'll surely get wet," said the fox.

So the gingerbread man hopped up on the fox's back, and the fox swam farther.

After a while the water got still deeper, and the fox spoke again.

"Hop up higher or you'll surely get wet," he said.

So the gingerbread man hopped up onto the fox's head, and that was a big mistake.

With a toss of his head,
the crafty fox flipped
the gingerbread man into
the air and, *snip! snap!*
into his mouth.

And that was the end of the gingerbread man.

The Husband Who Tried to Keep House

There was a man so mean and cross
that he never thought his wife
did anything right in the house.
He said he could do more work in
a day than his wife could do in three.

One evening during the hay-
harvesting season, he came home
scolding and fussing and grumbling.

"Here you sit about the house all day while I labor and sweat in the fields,"
he complained. "And yet you cannot even manage to have my supper ready on time.
A fine life! A fine wife!"

"There, there, dear love," said his sweet wife. "Tomorrow let's change our work.
I'll go out with the mowers to mow hay, and you shall stay at home
and mind the house."

The husband thought this was a splendid idea.

So early next morning, the wife took a scythe over her shoulder and went out into the hayfield with the mowers and began to mow. And the man stayed home to do the housework and care for their child.

First of all he was to churn the butter. But after he had churned a while, he became thirsty and went down in the cellar to tap a barrel of cider.

When his mug was only half full he heard the pig come into the kitchen overhead. Off he ran up the cellar steps to stop the pig from overturning the butter churn.

But when he got up he saw that the pig had already knocked the churn over and was rooting about and grunting while the cream ran all over the floor.

The man became so wild with rage that he quite forgot about the cider barrel. He ran at the pig as hard as he could and caught him, too. But the pig slipped out of his hands and ran out the door.

Then all at once the man remembered the cider barrel. But by the time he got back to the cellar every bit of cider had run out of the barrel.

Then he went into the dairy and found enough cream to fill the churn once more. So he began to churn again, for they had to have butter for dinner. But when he had churned a bit, he remembered that their milking cow was still shut up in the barn and hadn't had a bite to eat or a drop to drink all morning, though by now the sun was high.

Well, he thought it would take too long if he took the cow down to the meadow. So instead he decided to get her up on the housetop. The roof was thatched with sod and had a fine crop of grass growing there.

Now the house lay close up against a steep bank and the man thought he'd easily get the cow up if he laid a plank across from the bank to the roof.

But he still couldn't leave the churn, for his little baby was crawling about the floor. "If I leave the churn here the baby is sure to upset it," he said.

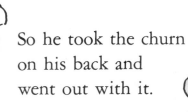

So he took the churn on his back and went out with it.

But then he thought he'd better water the cow before turning her loose on the roof to graze. So he took up a bucket to draw water out of the well. But as he stooped over the well, all the cream ran out of the churn, over his shoulders, and into the well.

When he finally got the cow on
the roof it was near dinner time,
and the man hadn't even finished
churning the butter yet.

But he thought he'd better
start the porridge water boiling.
He filled the pot with water and
hung it over the fire.

When he had done that, he remembered the cow on the roof and thought she might fall and break her legs or her neck. So he got up on the house to tie her up.

One end of the rope he tied around the cow and the other he slipped down the chimney.

He ran back down to the kitchen and tied the rope around his leg. He had to hurry for the water in the pot was already beginning to boil, and he still had to grind the oatmeal for the porridge. So he began to grind away.

OATS

But while he was hard at it, down fell the cow from the housetop. And as she fell she dragged the man up into the chimney.

There he stuck fast, while the poor cow hung halfway down the wall of the house. She was swinging between heaven and earth, for she could neither get down nor up.

Meanwhile, the man's wife, who was mowing in the field, waited and waited for her husband to call her home for dinner. But never a call came. At last she thought she'd waited long enough, and home she went.

When she got there and saw the cow hanging in such a bad way, she ran up and cut the rope in two with her scythe.

As she did this, down came her husband out of the chimney. And when his old wife came into the kitchen, she found him standing with his head in the porridge pot.

The next morning the man went back to mowing as usual.

"A fine wife! A fine life!" he said as he kissed his wife good-by, only this time he meant it. And never again did he complain that his wife sat around the house all day while he worked hard in the fields.